ELIVIA SAVADIER

WILL SHEILA SHARE?

A NEAL PORTER BOOK
ROARING BROOK PRESS
NEW YORK

For Julie Cash, with love.

Copyright © 2008 by Elivia Savadier
A Neal Porter Book
Published by Roaring Brook Press
Roaring Brook Press is a division of Holtzbrinck Publishing Holdings Limited Partnership
175 Fifth Avenue, New York, New York 10010

Distributed in Canada by H. B. Fenn and Company Ltd.

Library of Congress Cataloging-in-Publication Data:
Savadier, Elivia.
Will Sheila share? / by Elivia Savadier.
p. cm.
"A Neal Porter Book."
Summary: Nana helps teach her toddler granddaughter to share.
ISBN-13: 978-1-59643-289-5
ISBN-10: 1-59643-289-6
[1. Sharing—Fiction. 2. Grandparent and child—Fiction.] I. Title.
PZ7.S2584Wil 2008
2007010039

Roaring Brook Press books are available for special promotions and premiums.
For details contact: Director of Special Markets, Holtzbrinck Publishers.

First edition March 2008
Printed in China
2 4 6 8 10 9 7 5 3 1

Will Sheila share?

She will **not** share!

Not her bunny,

or her ball.

No, Sheila **will not** share.

"**Can** Sheila share?" asks Hana.

"Some of the time she can," says Jin.

"When she has a box of cereal,

she can share."

"When she eats green beans,

she can share."

Nana says, "She can share a hug

and a kiss."

Nana says, "Juice for me."

Nana says, "Juice for you."

Sheila says, "Berry for me!"

Sheila says, "Berry for you!"

"Now a berry for Jess," says Nana.

"NO!"
says Sheila.

Nana says,
"Look, Jess is sad."

Sheila says, "Berry for Jess!"

"Berry for Hana! Berry for Jin! Berry for Baby!"

Now Sheila will share!